Do Tell . . .
WHAT'S THAT
Smell?

Other books by
Sandy Bacon Harding

Goose on the Loose
A Stick A Stone and A Bone

Do Tell . . . WHAT'S THAT Smell?

by Sandy Bacon Harding
illustrated by Brenda Mickelson

Farm Adventure Series

Lion's Paw Books
Eagle Point, Oregon

Farm Adventure Series

Lion's Paw Books
A division of Coronet Books and Publications
P.O. Box 957, Eagle Point, OR 97524

Summary: Still adjusting to the death of her father and her new
home, Jenny learns about responsibility and forgiveness during
a church mishap.

Library of Congress Catalog Card number 97-092607
ISBN 1-890609-07-2

Contents

Written especially for ages
six to eleven.

Do Tell . . . What's That Smell? and other Farm Adventures, are based on true stories, many of which happened on a farm in southern Oregon.

1

Bessie's Escape

Jenny paused at the end of the brushy trail. Cherry blossoms littered the path to her grandparents' house. Wisps of steam rose off the old barn. She never saw this kind of stuff in the city. A duck squabble on the pond behind the farmhouse interrupted her thoughts.

Jenny almost didn't see the big black cow standing in the middle of the drive. "Oh great," she said, looking at the empty pasture. "Bessie, you're in trouble now."

Jenny still missed the city and especially her dad. Farm life was as opposite as you could get from Seaport. No movies, no malls and no sidewalks to rollerblade on. There were even more animals than people. But after Dad died, Mom said they had to move to Deer Point.

Jenny looked around for Grandpa. He was out of earshot in the upper pasture. She sucked in her breath as she slowly approached the cow. Why can't cows stay where they belong?

Jenny reached up and gingerly scratched the silken black face as the cow chewed her cud. She remembered what Grandpa had told her, "You've got to make them think you're in charge!" Building up courage, she grabbed the cow's halter. Bessie didn't move a muscle.

"Don't be rough, but be firm," she remembered Grandpa's words.

"Come on, Bessie, let's find Grandpa." As Jenny took that first step, the cow obediently followed. It worked!

Grandpa was bent over the old tractor. A red handkerchief dangled from the back pocket of his faded overalls. Before Jenny could say a word, Bessie laid her big head on Grandpa's shoulder. As he jumped back, his sweat-stained hat fell off. The fat cow grunted, giving off the smell of sweet grass.

"Bessie, what in tarnation are you doing up here?" Grandpa scolded. "And, youngun, you ought to make a little noise when you go sneaking up on people." He picked up his hat and shoved it down over silver hair. Grandpa always needed a haircut.

"She was just standing by the fence, Grandpa. I knew you'd want her back in her pasture," Jenny replied, somewhat hurt by his rough voice.

"I'm sorry, Jenny. It's just a bit uncanny when a body thinks he's alone and then feels that hot smelly breath." He nodded to the cow. "So you brought her up by yourself? We'll make a farmgirl out of you yet!"

Jenny winced. A farmgirl! Get real! she thought. The words almost came out.

Grandpa added, "Let's put her back before she gets into Grandma's flowers." They walked together as Bessie lumbered back to her pasture. Jenny picked up a small bucket of grain as they passed the shed.

"Carlos and Johnny are coming over today," Grandpa said.

"That's cool, Grandpa." Jenny was glad to talk about something else. "I guess this won't be a boring Saturday, after all."

Jenny wouldn't mind seeing Carlos, her cousin from Waterford. Johnny was another story. Johnny's real name was

Juan and he was a real pain-in-the-neck. On his last visit, he "borrowed" Jenny's camera. He used up a whole roll of film as he chased a poor rooster all over the barnyard.

Another time he dumped a can of sardines in the duck pond to see if they could swim.

When Jenny touched the pasture gate, it swung open. "Grandpa, look! It isn't even latched!" Jenny rattled the bucket as she walked through the gate. Bessie followed her right in.

"Well I'll be . . . I know I hooked it this morning," Grandpa said as he examined the latch. "That rascal's been getting out right regular."

"Are you learning some new tricks, Bessie?" Grandpa continued. "If you keep getting out, I'll have to put a lock on."

Grandpa always talked to the animals. Sometimes people wondered if he actually expected them to answer.

Jenny stuck her hand in the bucket of grain. "When's she going to have her calf?" she asked. She grimaced as

Bessie shoved her cold, wet nose into her hand.

"Any day now," Grandpa replied. "Maybe then she won't be so eager to get out. I guess she gets lonesome." As they left the pasture, he wiggled the gate to make sure it was latched.

Grandpa worried about the animals being lonesome. Jenny figured that he worried about her mom and her being lonesome too, before they moved to the farm. But sometimes Jenny got lonesome here, too. She missed her friends and the things she used to do. Would she ever get used to farm life?

2

Lamb Tails

Near the farmhouse, a duck slipped into some bushes looking for a secret place to nest. Jenny walked by, pretending not to see her. Ducks are funny that way. They just seem happier thinking no one knows where they are hiding.

Jenny joined Grams inside at the kitchen table. Grams put a hot oatmeal cookie in front of her and asked, "How's school going, Jenny? You'll be out for summer soon, won't you?"

Grams was OK. She always took time out to talk with Jenny, Grandpa, or anyone, for that matter. Usually the visit came with coffee and maybe pie or a cookie. Grandma wiped her hands on her blackberry-stained apron.

"Only a little over a month to go," Jenny said, licking crumbs off her lips.

The lazy sound of "Baa . . . baa" floated through the open window.

Jenny glanced out. "Look at Eunice, Grams. Looks like she's going to fall over!" The ewe was standing sideways on the hill across from the pond. She was as round as a ball, but that was because of her wool. The sheep shearer was coming today.

Grandpa said he liked to wait until around Easter for shearing. "Don't want them to get too cold," he had told Jenny.

The twin lambs butted Eunice as they nursed, almost lifting her off the ground. PeeWee was getting bigger, but he was still a lot smaller than Goliath. Jenny thought back to the day PeeWee was born. Jenny had found him stuck behind bales of hay and rescued him.

As the little lambs drank, their long black tails wagged limply. In a few minutes they bounced away as though they had springs on their hooves.

Jenny and Grams laughed at the playful lambs. "How come they're black instead of white like Eunice and Rambo?" Jenny asked. "And how come Rambo can't live with his family?"

Grams sat in the rocker and patted a space for Jenny to squeeze in. Grams

had a comfortable, ample lap, but
Jenny had outgrown it. Before long,
there wouldn't be room for both of
them in the chair at all. Fiddling with
Jenny's long dark braid, Grams replied,
"As for their being black, I always

wondered about that myself. The lambs are always born black. When we first got the young lambs, I thought I'd have some nice black yarn to spin. But by shearing time they've always turned white. They're Suffolk sheep and the only part that stays black are their faces and legs."

Shifting her weight she added, "Now Rambo is another story. Have you noticed that Grandpa never turns his back on him? That's because most rams can be mean and Rambo is no exception. You just can't trust them. Sometimes you might even see Grandpa carrying a stick if Rambo is in a particularly sour mood."

Grams continued, "We used to have an ornery ram when your dad was a youngster. That ram had me trapped in the garden once. Even though your dad was only about seven, he did some mighty sweet-talking and got the ram back to his pasture. Grandpa was real proud of him."

Jenny liked to hear stories about her dad, but it was still painful. She swallowed, then asked, "How come Grandpa wants the lambs' tails to fall off? It must hurt to have rubber bands on them."

"Gracious, child. You're going to get wrinkles worrying so much! As for the tail issue, you can see how much wool Eunice has. Well, it would be some mess if she had a tail to tend with, wouldn't it? And as for the bands, they don't bother the lambs one bit. The tails just fall off. In a few weeks you can go looking around the pasture and you're apt to find them."

"Maybe I could hang a lamb tail from my hat?" Jenny teased. "They'd make cool earrings too."

Her own words echoed in her mind. I'd die if my old friends heard me say that!

Jenny quickly added, "Well Johnny would think it was neat for a hat."

"Johnny would like that, I'm sure," Grandma said. "Just don't go giving him any more ideas. The last time he was here, he filled my wood box up with dried cow pies."

Jenny cringed. She would have to make sure Johnny washed his hands ten times before he touched her. To think that a year ago, she didn't even know that cow pie was just a polite name for manure.

"You're just full of ideas, Jenny. Now go get a little sunshine. Besides, I've got pies to finish." Grandma playfully shooed her outside.

3

Something's in the Shop

Jenny went to check on Henny Penny. The Banty hen paraded around with her half dozen chicks. They were little more than yellow balls of fluff with tiny brown stripes.

A shadow swooped across the chicken yard. Henny Penny clucked furiously as the chicks darted under her wings. Jenny looked up and saw that it was just a bird. That's weird, she thought.

Grandpa was picking up his tools when Jenny caught up with him.

"Grandpa, Henny Penny was acting really weird. You'd have thought someone shot at her the way she carried on when a bird flew over the chicken yard. The chicks got scared too and hid under her wings."

"Might'a been a Red Tail Hawk," Grandpa replied. "They come 'round here sometimes. They dive down and steal a chick if no one's watching. Henny Penny is a wise hen and she's teaching her younguns about the dangers of life. Them Banty chickens are real smart, not like the bigger ones. They even roost in trees instead of the henhouse. A 'coon will get the regular chickens, but not often them Bantys."

Jenny helped Grandpa carry the tools. "What's Grandma up to?" he asked.

"She's making pies for Easter supper at church. I think blackberry. She said picking time better come soon or she'll run out of frozen berries."

Grandpa's light blue eyes twinkled. "She makes the best pies around, that's for sure." Grandma's cooking was well known around Deer Point.

As Grandpa opened the shop door, they both heard it. A sound like paper rustling. Grandpa motioned for Jenny to be quiet. He turned on the lights. The noise stopped.

Grandpa looked around. He examined all the dark corners but couldn't find anything.

"Maybe some mice are moving in. We'll let Valentine sleep here tonight. That cat needs to get used to mousing," Grandpa said. Though Valentine wasn't even grown, she had already brought home a mouse or two.

Even country cats were different than city cats. In Seaport her best friend's cat liked to spend the entire day sunning herself in front of a window. Living in a high-rise, Snowflake rarely saw the outdoors, let alone a mouse.

The blast of a car horn stopped Jenny's thoughts. Three more blasts told Jenny that cousin Johnny had arrived.

A shaggy-haired six-year-old squirmed in the driver's seat of a minivan. He rolled down the window and shouted, "Jen-ny!"

Before Jenny could respond, he hollered again, "Jen-ny, come see me drive!"

4

The Visit

Aunt Maria came out of the house just as Grandpa and Jenny got to the van. "You know better than to play in cars!" she scolded Johnny.

"He's so excited to be here," Maria continued. Johnny jumped out of the van.

Jenny didn't know her cousins well. Carlos and his mom, Maria, were from Honduras. Jenny's uncle, Will, met her when he spent a year there on a missionary outreach. Carlos was four at the time. Jenny's uncle and Maria fell in love, married and moved back to Oregon. Then they had Johnny.

Grandpa affectionately gave Johnny a knuckle-burn on his head. "There's a lot of fun things

to do around here, Johnny," he said. "You don't need to be playing in cars."

"Hi, Johnny," Jenny said. He grabbed her hand and grinned. Jenny flinched as she remembered the cow pie incident. "Let's go wash up," she added.

"OK, you're the boss," Johnny said.

Jenny felt guilty for thinking he was such a pest.

Aunt Maria and Grandpa followed Jenny and Johnny inside. The sweet aroma of blackberries floated through the whole house. Grams tucked in a few loose strands of hair.

"This will warm everyone up," Grandma said as she set steaming cups of cocoa on the table. Aunt Maria's dark eyes danced from Jenny to Grandpa as "hellos" were exchanged. Johnny twirled around Jenny.

"Jenny, you've grown so much! You must be taller than I am," Maria said.

Jenny gave Aunt Maria a hug. It felt good to be taller than a grownup.

"How's the city, Maria?" Grandpa asked. Jenny sighed at Grandpa's words. To Grandpa, anyplace with traffic lights and sidewalks was a city. "Didn't Carlos come?" Grandpa added.

Johnny rushed back over to Grandpa's arms.

"Someone call me?" Carlos stuck a comb in his pocket as he came from the hallway. He ran a hand over his slicked-back hair.

Jenny looked at her handsome cousin. He was a whole head taller than his mom. Sometimes she wished they weren't related.

"Hi, Carlos. How's school going?" Grandpa asked.

Jenny's cheeks reddened as she managed a "Hello, Carlos." Why couldn't she think of anything to say to him?

Grandpa eyed some pies sitting on the counter. "Hi, Lovey, looks like

you've been busy." He stretched a long
arm toward a pie.

"Not till tomorrow," she teased,
tapping his fingers. As Grams went
back to the stove, Grandpa dipped his
finger in some spilled pie filling and
quickly licked it off.

Jenny pointed to his mustache and whispered, "Grandpa, you've got berries on your . . ."

Just then Grams turned around. Grandpa quickly licked his mustache and winked at the kids.

"How's Bessie doing?" Grams asked Grandpa, seeming not to notice. Turning to Johnny, she added, "Bessie's going to have a calf any day now, Johnny. Maybe even while you're here."

"She's getting restless," Grandpa replied. "Got out of her pasture again. I don't know how she does it."

Jenny said, "Grandpa thinks there are mice in the shop."

"Might be after the bag of grain I left there," Grandpa added.

Grams looked thoughtful. "Could be squirrels. Remember a couple of years ago when the corn was disappearing so fast? That was before you moved here, Jenny. Anyway, your Grandpa parked himself on a stool watching the barn until he caught squirrels sneaking in and out. Corn was pouching out their cheeks as they scampered away." Grams laughed. "They got so fat that year, they could hardly walk."

"I wanna see the squirrels," Johnny said.

"The squirrels are fat in Seaport, too," Jenny said. "They have vending machines for squirrel food in the park and everybody likes to feed them."

"Those squirrels wouldn't survive around here, that's for sure," Grandpa said. "Some winters, food can be scarce as hen's teeth."

"Come on, Jenny. Let's go see the squirrels," Johnny insisted.

"Why don't the three of you go and find some squirrels—just don't bring them in the house!" Grandma said.

Jenny, Johnny and Carlos went outside. Jenny glanced at Bessie's pasture as they walked by. "Shhh . . ." Jenny whispered. "Look!"

Carlos stared at the black cow. "What's she doing?"

"Is she gonna have her baby?" Johnny asked in a loud whisper.

5

Bessie's Secret

Jenny stared. "Unreal!" she whispered. There was Bessie—down on her knees by the gate, rubbing her nose against the latch. "Let's see what she does," Jenny said.

The kids hid behind the van and watched to see what Bessie would do next.

Bessie rubbed and rubbed, working on the latch. Then . . . the gate swung open and out she walked. She lumbered up behind the shop.

"So that's how she is getting out," Jenny said. "Grandpa couldn't figure it out."

"It looks like she knows exactly where she's going," Carlos said. He took the lead as the three kids followed the cow, keeping out of sight. Bessie stopped at the corner of the shop and nosed the ground. They sneaked closer. Bessie lifted her head . . . bits of grain fell from her nose.

Where did that come from? Jenny wondered. Her eyes followed the specks to a small mound of grain near the corner of the shop.

"We have to put her back in the pasture," Jenny said. "Otherwise, she might get into Grandma's flowers."

Jenny took a deep breath as she grabbed Bessie's halter. She gave a tug, but this time the cow wouldn't budge. Jenny pulled and pulled. Why did this have to happen in front of Carlos? Jenny thought miserably.

Carlos grabbed the other side of the halter and pulled. Johnny pushed from behind. Bessie swished her tail and got Johnny right in the face.

"That's yucky!" Johnny said.

Bessie just stood there, calmly chewing her cud. Finally Jenny said, "We'd better get Grandpa."

Grandpa didn't feel like wrestling with Bessie either. "If a cow don't want to move, she ain't moving," he told the kids.

They all went to the barn. "This alfalfa is her favorite," Grandpa said. Leafy dark green flakes flew everywhere as he separated a wedge off a bale. He handed it to Carlos.

When Bessie saw the hay, she followed Carlos straight to the pasture. Jenny told Grandpa about Bessie and the gate and about the pile of grain near the shop.

"So that's how she's getting out!" Grandpa said. "I wish you had a camera. We could send it to Amazing Animals." He wrapped a piece of twine around the latch. "That ought to stop her for now."

They went to the shop. Inside, a feedbag was propped in the corner. Grandpa moved it and a trail of grain spilled out. It disappeared through a crack in the floor. "Well, that solves the grain mystery," Grandpa muttered. Then they heard the rustling sound. Something was under the shop!

Grandpa picked up a flashlight and whispered, "Come on, kids, I think we found our mice."

Poking around, he discovered where something had dug under the shop. "This can't be mice," he whispered. "Too big."

Getting down on his hands and knees, he shined the light into the darkness. Four eyes glowed back.

6

"No More Pets!"

Grandpa said, "Look! Baby skunks!" He quickly moved the flashlight around, looking for the mother. He didn't want to surprise her, that's for sure. "Skunks usually sleep during the day because they're nocturnal. That means they do their roaming and eating at night. The mother must be napping someplace else." He carefully picked up one of the babies.

"I want one!" Johnny wailed.

"They're so cute," Jenny said. "They look like tiny black and white kittens!"

"Don't seem to have their scent yet," Grandpa remarked. He picked up the second one and stroked its soft fur. "Let's surprise Grams. I heard that skunks make good pets."

"My friend has a pet skunk," Carlos said. "It's cool."

Jenny noticed a slight smell, kind of musty, but it didn't seem strong. "I don't know, Grandpa. Grams is kinda funny about what makes a good pet. Dad used to tell me that you were always bringing something home."

"She'll like 'em, you'll see," he said, sticking them under his coat.

The four of them trailed back to the farmhouse. Johnny bounced up and down, half running, half skipping, in front of them.

"Wait till you see! Wait till you see!" Johnny hollered as he burst through the door. Grandpa followed, with Jenny and Carlos close behind.

Grandpa proudly unbuttoned his coat and pulled out the babies. "Look, Lovey. Look what we found."

Grams jumped out of her rocker so fast her gray bun wobbled "What are you thinking, George? Skunks in the house!" Her dark blue eyes flashed.

Grandpa tried to talk Grams into keeping them. She interrupted, "George, you love animals, I love animals. But there's a limit. They're still skunks and I don't want them in the house! Please take them back outside!"

The room was silent as Grandpa stroked the soft fur. "We could get them descented," he pleaded.

Grandma said, "We'll have to discuss that later, George. They're smelling up the place!"

Maria picked up her coat and said, "We'd better get going. We'll see you at church tomorrow."

"Can I spend the night, pul-eeze, pul-eeze?" Johnny pleaded as he tugged at Grandma.

"If your mom says it's OK and your grandpa gets rid of those skunks!" Grams said.

"You can stay only if you promise to be good," Maria said. Then she told Grams, "We can pick him up tomorrow."

Maria and Carlos left. Jenny wished it were Carlos who got to stay.

"Now, George, will you please take those skunks back outside?" Grams said. "And Jenny, can you keep an eye on Johnny? Sometimes your grandpa doesn't notice things 'till it's too late."

"I guess so, Grams," Jenny said.

Jenny, Grandpa and Johnny left with the skunks. Jenny heard Grams open a window and mutter something about skunk smell.

Grandpa put the skunks back under the shop. "They would have made good pets, I reckon." Though the skunks were cute, it didn't surprise Jenny that Grams didn't want them as pets.

7

Shearing Time

A beat-up white truck with wood siderails pulled into the driveway. A bowlegged man in a cowboy hat and dirty jeans stepped out. "Hi, Leo," Grandpa said.

"Howdy, George!" the man bellowed out.

The man fumbled around in the back of the truck. He pulled out something that looked like a giant hair cutter with a long cord. He flipped a couple pieces of red twine over his back and started up to the barn. Grandpa coaxed Eunice over with a can of grain. The curious lambs followed.

Johnny squatted on the ground. The man petted Eunice. In one easy motion, he had her half-sitting, half lying, on her back. She didn't move or make a sound as he held her head between his knees. "When you get them in this position, they feel helpless and won't move a bit," he said.

The man made some swipes down her stomach, then sort of rolled the wool off her back with the clippers.

"It looks just like she's taking off a coat," Johnny said.

"She looks so different," Jenny said.

The man finished up with a little special clipping around her tail. The whole thing didn't take ten minutes. He rolled the wool up into a ball and tied it with the twine.

"You can come get your pair of geese whenever you like," Grandpa told the man.

"Thanks, George. Got one more place to go today. I'll see you later," he told Grandpa as he put his tools away. He tossed the wool into the back of his truck and drove off to the next farm.

They watched the lambs sniff their mother. Eunice sure looked different.

Johnny wandered off to see if Bessie had had her calf.

"What did you mean about the geese, Grandpa?" Jenny asked.

"We try to barter whenever it works out," Grandpa said. "He wanted geese, and I wanted sheepshearing, so we traded."

Jenny thought she better check on Johnny. She found him near the shop.

"It's getting late, Johnny," Jenny said. "Let's go inside."

She walked Johnny back to the farmhouse. "I'll see you tomorrow, Grams," Jenny said. "Johnny, you be good."

Grandpa was on the porch, taking off his boots. Jenny said, "I've got to go, Grandpa. See you later."

"Bye, honey," Grandpa said.

Jenny gave him a hug. She noticed his clothes still smelled a little like skunk. Grandpa went inside.

Jenny started walking home. She got as far as the shop when she heard Grandpa outside again. She turned to wave just as he hung his shirt on a hook on the porch.

Grandpa didn't see her. "So much bother," he muttered to himself. "It's only a little skunk smell."

Jenny gasped. Grandpa was standing on the porch in his long-underwear!

8

Easter Surprise

The next morning, Mom called "Come on, Jenny, we'll be late. You get the cake and I'll bring the Bibles."

"I hope it gets warmer," Jenny said, grabbing her coat. She picked up the chocolate chip cake and followed her mother to the car.

As they pulled into the church parking lot, Jenny rolled down the window. "Hi Bethany," she called out to her friend.

"Hi, Jenny. Hurry! They're having games upstairs," Bethany said. Jenny jumped out as soon as the car stopped.

"Wait a minute, you two. I can't carry the cake and the Bibles," Mom said.

"Sorry, Mom," Jenny said, taking the Bibles.

"I'll carry the cake," Bethany said.

Her mom smiled. Jenny knew her mom was glad she was making friends. It hadn't been easy for either of them. First losing dad, then moving to Deer Point and Mom having to get a job.

Grandpa, Grams and Johnny drove up. Jenny looked at the old truck her grandparents drove. She noticed many other old cars and trucks in the parking lot. Jenny sighed. In the country, people didn't seem so concerned about everything being new.

"Hi!" Jenny called out as the truck stopped.

"I gotta go see someone," Johnny said as he jumped out of the truck. He had a shoebox in his arms.

"Hello, girls. Hi Lydia," Grams said to Jenny's mom. "Could you help me with these pies before Pa here sticks his finger in one. George, can you bring the salad?"

"Are you sure you can trust me?" Grandpa said. He looked around at the full parking lot. "I hope there's plenty of food."

Jenny and Bethany ran inside. Carlos was already there with Uncle Will and Aunt Maria.

"Your cousin is really cute," Bethany whispered.

"Remember, we're not related by blood!" Jenny whispered back. "Let's go say 'hi'."

The two girls went over to Carlos. Jenny said, "Carlos, this is my friend, Bethany."

"Hi, Bethany," Carlos said.

Bethany mumbled, "Glad you could come."

Jenny looked at her friend. Bethany's hair looked even blonder against her red face. Jenny had never seen Bethany embarrassed.

"Did Johnny stay out of trouble last night?" Carlos asked.

"Far as I could tell. The sheep got sheared and that was cool. Then he kept checking on Bessie."

The church was filled with people and the heat was on. Everyone was standing around talking. It was getting warm. Actually, it was getting stuffy. Grandpa loosened his tie as sweat trickled down his neck.

Jenny and Bethany took Carlos to meet the rest of the older kids. The choir members were getting in their places. Conversation floated around, then, without warning, stopped. People began whispering. Suddenly someone blurted out, "I smell a skunk!"

Oh, no! Jenny sucked in her breath. Could it be the skunks from yesterday?

Carlos looked around between the pews. Bethany ran to the window to see if a skunk was outside. Jenny looked at Grandpa. He had a funny look on his face. People started moving away from him.

How embarrassing! Grandpa smells like a skunk!

After a little stuttering, Grandpa explained, "They were just babies. No smell, it didn't seem, and they didn't spray."

One guy came over and gave Grandpa a friendly punch on the arm.

Carlos and Bethany joined Jenny. Bethany whispered, "Your grandpa is so funny!" She grinned.

Jenny tried to smile, but it looked more like a grimace. For sure, this would never happen in the city!

Grandpa told everyone his skunk story. "And Lovey here, made me strip on the porch. I just hope no one got pictures of me standing outside in my longjohns!"

Jenny didn't say a word.

Then she noticed the kidding was friendly, and Grandpa was even joking back. Even though Grandpa was different, these people really did like him.

"I can't figure it out. I even took another shower this morning," Grandpa said. "The smell musta got in my pores!"

Harley, an old-timer, said in a cracking voice, "Skunk smell is like that. First ya think it's gone, then it ain't. Kind'a like garlic, stays with ya for awhile."

A commotion broke out near the storage closet. A trio of young boys stood by the open door. "Let me see!" one boy said.

"No, it's my turn!" another said, tugging on a shoebox.

"Now look what you done!" Johnny wailed as the shoebox dropped to the floor.

Johnny went flying through the sanctuary holding the empty shoebox. The crowd parted as the familiar flash of black and white streaked by.

9

Forgiveness

Carlos took off after Johnny. The piano player jumped up on a bench, swished her skirt and screamed. Several older ladies squealed as they quickly shuffled out of the sanctuary. The skunks ran across the music platform with Johnny right behind them. The drums and cymbals crashed to the floor as Johnny dove at the skunks.

Pastor Jackson said, "Please, everybody stay calm."

It was anything but calm. Women were huddled together wringing their hands. Some were jumping up and down. Babies were crying. Several kids, mostly boys, were running after Johnny.

The crowd parted like waves, as the skunks, followed by Johnny, looked for an escape. Carlos was waving his arms. Finally, the skunks escaped through the open door. Carlos stopped Johnny at the door.

Grams called Johnny to her side. "Johnny, why in the world would you bring skunks to church?"

The empty shoebox hung limply from Johnny's hand. He looked at Grandma, then at Grandpa, and said, "I knew that Mr. Ingram would be here. He could take the skunks to his animal hospital and take away their smell. Then they could be pets."

Aunt Maria and Uncle Will came and got Johnny.

Jenny went over to Grams and said, "I'm sorry I didn't say something. I should have watched Johnny better yesterday. Especially when he was hanging around the shop. Then when I saw the shoebox . . ." Jenny hung her head. This is so embarrassing.

Grams put her arm around Jenny. "When you have a job to do, you need to use good judgement."

"I'm really sorry, Grandma," Jenny said.

Grandma put her arm around Jenny. "Growing up is not easy, Jenny. But when we do make mistakes, people who care about us will still forgive us."

The lady at the piano played a few chords. The choir tried to sing, but people were fanning the air. Some pinched their noses and everyone was making faces. Finally, Pastor Jackson said, "The sun is coming out. I think an outdoor Easter service is just what the Lord ordered." Everyone was chuckling. Some even poked Grandpa in the ribs.

Even though Jenny had heard the Easter message many times before, it had new meaning today. The pastor explained what Easter represented. She heard about forgiveness and that Jesus died that we might have life.

After church and supper, Bowmer O'Toole came over to Grandpa. He ran his hand through his thinning dark hair and said, "George, don't you go making pets out of any more skunks. We'll never forget this Easter!"

Grandpa replied, "You're just jealous 'cause you don't have wild critters on your place, Bowmer. Makes life interesting."

Does it ever, Jenny thought.

10

Bessie's Last Escape

Jenny rode home with Grams and Grandpa. As they neared the farm, Grandpa checked to make sure that Bessie was still in the pasture. She wasn't.

As soon as the truck stopped, Jenny hopped out and ran to the shop. No

Bessie. She looked towards the barn. Not there either.

"Here she is," Grandpa called out. She was standing in a clump of tall grass near Grandma's flowers. It didn't look like she had done any damage yet.

"At least I know how she gets out. Johnny must have visited her again yesterday. Jenny, we'll change that latch tomorrow when you come over after school."

As they got closer, Bessie gave a soft moo and nudged a shiny black lump on the ground beside her. It moved.

By now, Grams had caught up with them. "Well, mercy be . . ." she exclaimed, as the wet calf struggled to its feet. It tried to steady itself as Bessie roughly licked its face.

Jenny stood in awe admiring the newborn calf. "It has cow licks all over!" she remarked.

Grandpa took Jenny's hand and said, "Another new life. Yup, Easter is a great day for a new life." Squeezing her hand, he said, "I'll take this life any day, skunks and all."

"Me too, Grandpa." Jenny sighed. She knew sometimes she'd miss the city but the farm was filled with more surprises than she ever expected and a whole lot of love and forgiveness, too.

Other Farm Adventures

ISBN 1-890609-05-6
$6.95

Book I

Goose on the Loose
By Sandy Bacon Harding
Illustrated by Debra Warford

Grandma and Grandpa have a peaceful farm in Deer Point. That changes when an intruder tries to move in on the pond. Andy the farm goose is sure he can't fly. Nevertheless, he finds himself airborne and ends up lost and surrounded by angry wild geese. Lucy, his mate, is heartsick, Grandpa can't find him. What will Andy do?

Both books are available from your favorite bookstore

or directly from the publisher.
$6.95 each + $1.50 shipping

Ask to have it autographed!

ISBN 1-890609-08-0
$6.95

Book II

A Stick A Stone and A Bone
By Sandy Bacon Harding
Illustrated by Brenda Mickelson

Jenny's world crashes when her dad dies and Mom says they have to move. They leave their comfortable high-rise in the city to live on a small farm in Deer Point.

Instead of movies, skating and malls, this weekend is filled with milking, cheese making and the difficult birth of a lamb. Then Jenny notices something strange. Things begin to disappear, then show up in the oddest places. Jenny is determined to solve the mystery and in doing so actually saves a life.

Coronet Books and Publications
PO Box 957
Eagle Point, OR 97524
e-mail: lions-paw@ccountry.net

Do Tell . . . What's That Smell? was inspired by a real event that occured during the time the author's husband pastored a church in Eagle Point Oregon.

Sandy Bacon Harding, grandmother of twelve, began writing stories while she and her family lived on a farm in Eagle Point, Oregon. All the stories in the Farm Adventure Series are based on true events. She and her husband, Gary, live in rural southern Oregon.

Brenda Mickelson is a wife and mother of four children: two at home, one in college and a married daughter in England. She graduated from Pacific Lutheran University with a Bachelor of Fine Arts degree. She and her husband, Dan, pastor a church in Medford, Oregon.